QED Understanding... **Bereavement**

A Place in My Heart

Copyright © QED Publishing 2007

First published in the UK in 2007 by
QED Publishing
A Quarto Group company
226 City Road
London EC1V 2TT
www.qed-publishing.co.uk

A catalogue record for this book is available
from the British Library.

ISBN 978 1 84538 693 1

Written by Annette Aubrey
Edited by Sarah Medina
Designed by Alix Wood
Illustrated by Patrice Barton
Consultancy by David Hart

Publisher Steve Evans
Creative Director Zeta Davies
Senior Editor Hannah Ray

Printed and bound in China

A Place in My Heart

Annette Aubrey

Illustrated by

Patrice Barton

QED Publishing

QED

"Ring, ring!" went the bell at Andrew's school.
It was hometime, but Andrew sighed.
He didn't want to go home right now.
His house felt so gloomy inside.

4

"My dad is really unhappy
And last night I heard Mummy cry.
We are all feeling so very sad
Because, last week, Grandad died."

Andrew's Dad was at the school gates.
Andrew told him, "I feel so bad.
I can't believe that Grandad died.
Why did he leave us, Dad?"

My heart feels so sad and empty,
And my tummy is churning inside.
Things won't ever be the same again.
I want Grandad by my side.

Just then, Andrew saw a ladybird
Creeping quietly up the wall.
"Dad! Grandad loved all ladybirds.
He showed me how they'd crawl...

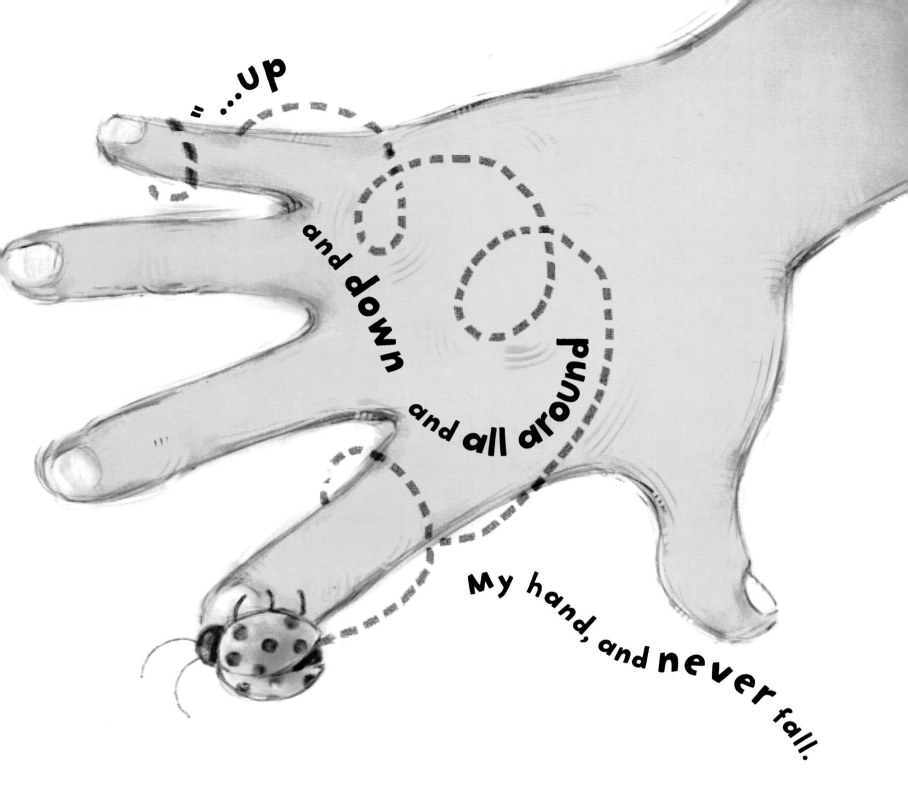

" ...up and down and all around

My hand, and never fall.

Now who will teach me all these things?
Oh, Dad. It's not fair at all!"

Dad gave Andrew a **big** bear hug.

I know that you're sad, my son.
All of these feelings are perfectly normal;
This is natural for everyone.

"When you have lost someone you love,
You are bound to feel terribly glum.
Yes, all of these feelings are normal,
When someone you love has gone."

Back at home, young Andrew's mum
Took Andrew's hands in her own.
"It's hard to know that Grandad's died,
And hard to feel all alone.

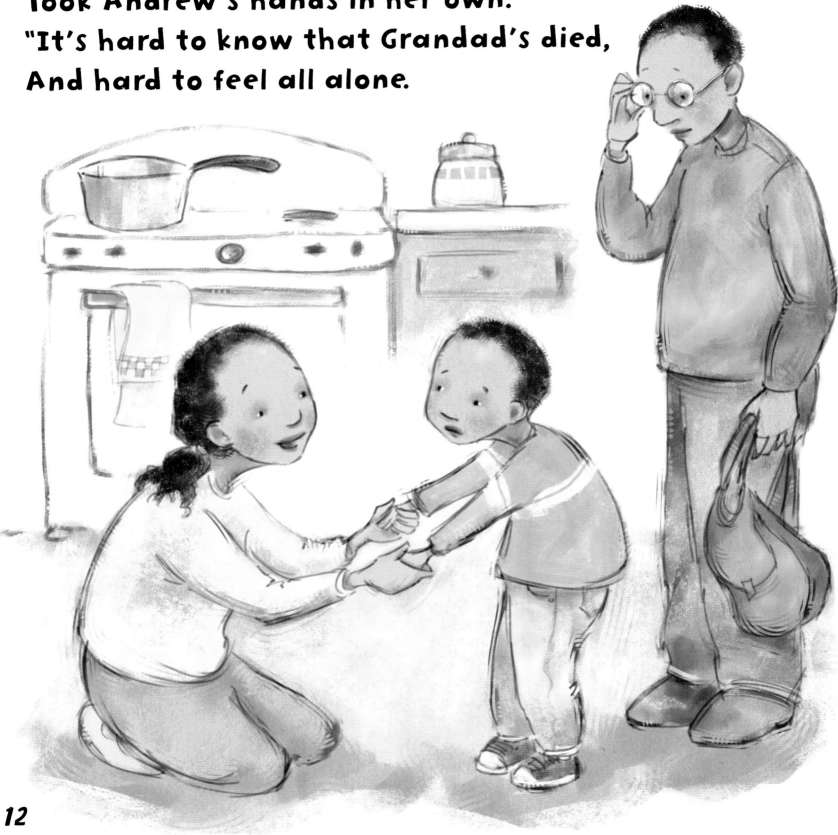

"Both Daddy and I do understand.
We, too, have cried our tears.

Let's face this sadness together," said Mum,
As she drew her little boy near.

14

So they all sat down at the table
In front of a wonderful spread.
They talked about Grandad's favourite things
And laughed at the things he'd said.

Dad said, "Look at these photos of Grandad.
Let's look at them here on the floor."
And the three of them sat and remembered
The grandad they all had adored.

They told many more Grandad stories,
And they laughed and cried and sighed.
They sort of felt Grandad was with them
Even though they knew that he'd died.

18

They felt him **deep inside**
their hearts,
So very deep inside.

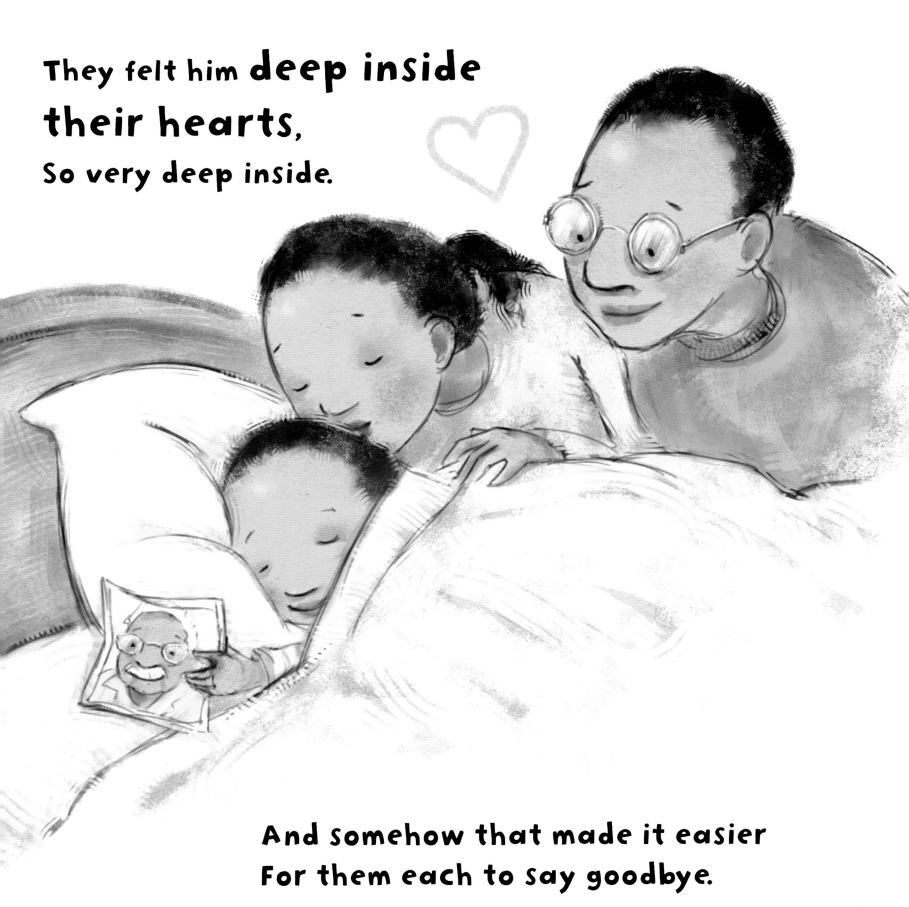

And somehow that made it easier
For them each to say goodbye.

Time came, time went
for Andrew.

And then, one sunny day,
The doorbell rang
   and Andrew's friend
Invited him to play.

The two friends ran in the garden.
They **jumped** and they **laughed**
and they **played**.

Then they quietly watched the ladybirds.
They had such a **wonderful day**.

"My grandad showed me many things,"
Said Andrew. "He was cool!
He taught me lots about ladybirds
And helped me out with school.

"And even though I still miss him,
He will never be far away.

Because Grandad said
when you love someone
They have a place in
your heart always."

23

NOTES FOR PARENTS AND TEACHERS

- Look at the front cover of the book together. Talk about the picture. Can your children guess what the book is going to be about?
- Explain to your children that when someone we love has died, we can experience a lot of different feelings, including sadness, fear, loneliness, anger and deep pain. Everyone has their own set of feelings, all of which are normal and right for them.
- Turn to pages 4 and 5. Ask your children how they think Andrew is feeling.
- On page 6, Andrew's dad is waiting to walk Andrew home from school. Ask your children how they think this makes Andrew feel.
- On page 7, Andrew describes how his body is feeling. Children are generally quite attuned to their bodies and will often describe how they are feeling and their emotions by saying things such as "I have got a tummy ache". Ask your children where they feel different emotions — sadness, happiness or anger — in their bodies.
- On page 8, Andrew sees a ladybird, which then reminds him of his grandad. Ask your children how they think Andrew is feeling now. Have his feelings changed? If so, why? Explain that it is normal for feelings to change a lot during sad times.
- On pages 10 and 11, Dad reassures Andrew that all his feelings are natural and normal. Ask your children how they think Andrew feels when his dad gives him a hug. If Andrew was their friend, what would they say to help him to feel better?
- On pages 12 and 13, Andrew's mum explains that she and Andrew's dad, too, are very sad about Andrew's grandad dying. How do your children think that this makes Andrew feel? How do they think Andrew feels when his mum says, "Let's face this sadness together"?

- On page 14, Andrew chooses a dinner that his grandad would have liked. Ask your children why they think Andrew does this.
- On page 15, Andrew and his parents have dinner together, and remember Grandad fondly. Ask your children if they think that the family's feelings have changed now and, if so, how and why.
- As Andrew and his family look at photos of Grandad and talk about him on pages 16 to 18, they have lots of different feelings. Remind your children that it is normal for feelings to go up and down a lot during these times, and that it is helpful to express all their different feelings, whether they seem "good" or "bad".
- On page 19, Andrew and his parents feel that Grandad is deep inside their hearts. Ask your children what they think this means. How do they think this makes Andrew and his parents feel? Why do they think feeling Grandad in their hearts makes it a little easier for them to say goodbye to Grandad?
- On pages 20 and 21, time has passed, and Andrew and his friend have a wonderful day playing. This is a sign that Andrew's grief has also moved on. Ask your children how they think Andrew is feeling now? Do they think that he still feels sad about his grandad?
- On pages 22 and 23, Andrew remembers good things about his grandad as he talks to his friend. Ask your children what they think Andrew means when he says that his grandad will never be far away? How do they think that someone can live in a person's heart? How can you tell if someone is in your heart, and how would it feel?